JUMP THE SHARK
& THE PIRATE

WRITTEN & ILLUSTRATED BY:
E. DARWIN HARTSHORN

Dr. Jellybrain is not **Jump the Shark's** only foe. Let me tell you about **Cut Lass, the Pirate Princess**.

As the sun set on the Chronon Sea, the golden sky made the water look like liquid fire, dancing and blazing. And fire and smoke belched forth from the cannons of the **Sea Dog's Sword**, the ship of Cut Lass, the Pirate Princess, as they attacked a merchant vessel.

Suddenly, the *Sea Dog's Sword* lurched to one side, as though she had been shot!

"To arms!" Cut Lass shouted to her sea dogs. "We do be boarded by **Jump the Shark**, who be said to guard the magical **Pearl of McGuffin!**"

She drew her swords and rushed below deck to fight Jump.

Jump the Shark stood next to a hole in the hull, water pouring in. He did not say a word, for sharks cannot breath air, but he smiled. It was already too late for the *Sea Dog's Sword*.

Cut Lass tried to attack Jump, but with her ship filling with water, the shark easily dodged her strike.

Trapped in a sinking ship, the pirate closed her eyes and resigned herself to death.

But lights began to bubble up from the deep...

When she opened her eyes, she found herself on the seafloor, able to breathe water! Sera Mermaid floated beside her, the Pearl of McGuffin in one hand.

"I have given you and your dogs the power to live beneath the waves," the mermaid said. "Now please dedicate your new lives to good."

Jump the Shark was *not* happy.

"I'm new to this hero thing," Jump said, "but I thought we were supposed to stop the bad guys, not rescue them!"

"Just as you are sworn to valor," Sera Mermaid said, "I am sworn to mercy. I am bound to seek the good of the pirates even as I sought *your* good."

While Jump and Sera bickered, Cut Lass stalked over and seized the Pearl of McGuffin. "Here be booty fit for a Pirate Princess!" she crowed, raising it above her head.

The magic of the Pearl surrounded the pirate. It gathered the pieces of her sunken ship and knit them back together.

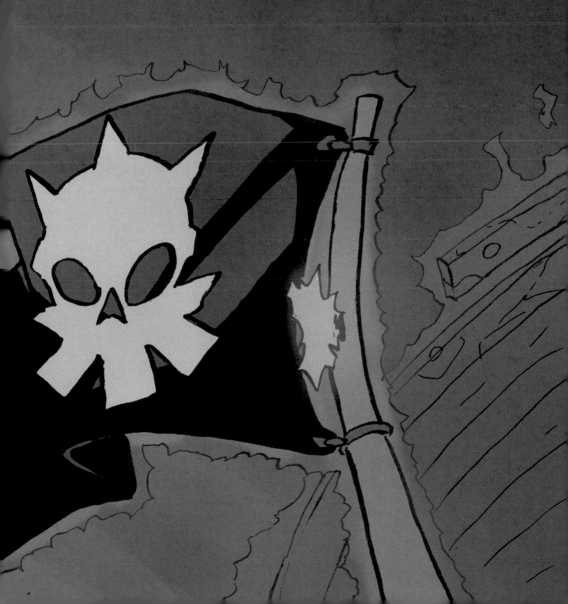

Jump and Sera turned from their argument and rushed towards the Pearl to get it back. But before they could reach it, Cut Lass waved her hand and a fragment of the *Sea Dog's Sword* scooped them up and sealed them away in the hold.

"At least she didn't kill us," Jump said.

"Nor could she," Sera said. "The Pearl can add powers or change powers. It cannot take powers away. She cannot kill us with the Pearl."

Light entered the hold as a door opened. Sea dogs stood in the door, swords drawn. "Arr!" they said. "Maybe the Pearl can't kill ye, but our swords can kill ye just fine!"

Jump wasted no time. With a shout and a fierce grin, he rushed the pirates.

With strength and speed born of Dr.
Jellybrain's mad science and the Pearl's
strange magic, Jump easily avoided the
weapons of the Sea Dogs.

"This way!" he shouted to Sera. "Let's put an
end to this nonsense!"

The pirate princess floated above the quarterdeck, sword in one hand, Pearl in the other, using magic to redesign her sunken vessel.

Jump seized her second sword, which lay on the deck, and charged at the pirate with a big, toothy smile on his face.

Even with the power of the Pearl, Cut Lass was not as fast or strong as Jump, but the pirate had years of training and experience with the sword, and the shark had almost none.

He swung his weapon wildly at the pirate,
and she brushed aside attack after attack
with small, efficient movements.

She barely seemed to be trying.

She pointed her sword at the charging shark, and a beam of energy burst from the blade and transfixed him.

Jump the Shark began to cough and choke.

He tried to say "But the Pearl can't be used to kill!" But he couldn't get the words out.

The Pirate Princess seemed to understand the sputtering shark just fine. "I did not use the Pearl to kill ye, shark," she said. "I gave ye the power to breathe air! Air and not water. Ye do be drownin'!"

Sera Mermaid rushed to Jump's side as he gasped for air deep beneath the sea.

Unfortunately, the pirate rushed toward the two of them at the same time, ready to strike the final blow to mermaid or shark...

Jump parried her strike at the last moment.

He couldn't swing his sword fast enough to hit the pirate. He could barely swing it at all now that he was drowning. With her next attack, Cut Lass would either strike down Jump, or strike down Sera Mermaid, and there was nothing the shark could do to stop it.

Whatever he chose to do next, it had to end the fight, and it had to work despite Jump's lack of skill.

Jump lunged, driving the point of his sword towards the Pearl.

Cut Lass tried to stop him. But she had expected another attack on her body, and she was too confident in her skill. Her defense cut through empty water.

The sword split the Pearl into seven shards. Light, sound, and force blasted out from the point of impact, tearing at the ship, the Pearl shards, the pirate, the shark, and the mermaid in a violent rainbow of destruction.

Jump blacked out.

Jump woke. Sera held a glowing shard of the pearl over him.

"I have given you a mermaid's breathing," she said, "both water and air alike, that no piece of the Pearl may again be used to drown you."

"What of the pirate princess?" Jump asked.

"Her sea dogs bore her away," Sera replied.

The sun began to rise behind the crystal spire. A new day began in the Chronon Sea.

THE END

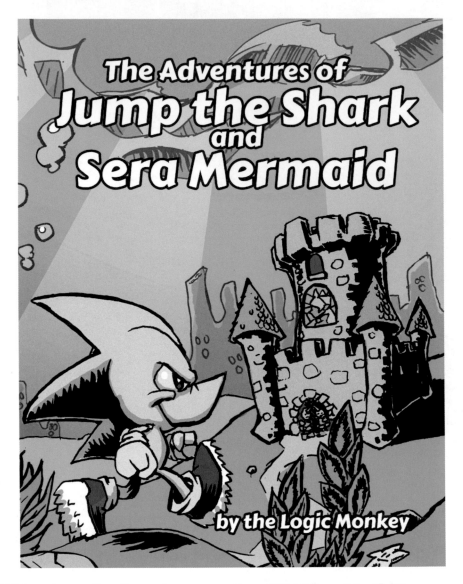

The Adventures of Jump the Shark and Sera Mermaid

by the Logic Monkey

The book that began it all! The Evil Dr. Jellybrain kidnaps a baby shark and uses training and mad science to turn him into a super-soldier for evil. Will Jump the Shark be able to wrest the mystical Pearl of McGuffin from Sera Mermaid? Will he be able to overcome his dark master? Find out in this fun-packed five minute adventure!

This page is reserved to talk about the thrilling seqel to *Jump the Shark and the Pirate Princess*. Since I haven't written it yet, here's a pixel art print test for a different series Jump the Shark might appear in. That also means this copy is an early edition, and there are probably some typos I've missed, if you want to try and catch me out. - *E. Darwin Hartshorn*

For the Short Stuff, and for Dan's kid

Published by:
E. Darwin Hartshorn: the Irrepressible Logic Monkey
logic.monkey@protonmail.com

About E. Darwin Hartshorn:

Hi! Last year I sat down to read my kid a book and realized "this could be a little more awesome." So I tried making my own kids' books with action, adventure, sharks, and (now) pirates.

You can follow my adventures in making kids' media at logicmonkey.media, and check out Jump the Shark stuff at:

logicmonkey.media/jump

Made in the USA
Coppell, TX
15 July 2023

19177577R00024